# Don't forget, Lara!

Julia Green

Illustrated by Giuditta Gaviraghi

A & C Black • London

White Wolves series consultant: Sue Ellis,
Centre for Literacy in Primary Education

This book can be used in the White Wolves Guided Reading
programme by more advanced readers in Year 2

First published 2010 by
A & C Black Publishers Ltd
36 Soho Square, London, W1D 3QY

www.acblack.com

Text copyright © 2010 Julia Green
Illustrations copyright © 2010 Giuditta Gaviraghi

The rights of Julia Green and Giuditta Gaviraghi to be identified
as the author and illustrator of this work has been asserted by them
in accordance with the Copyrights, Designs and Patents Act 1988.

ISBN 978-1-4081-1374-5

A CIP catalogue for this book is available from the British Library.

All rights reserved. No part of this publication may be
reproduced in any form or by any means – graphic, electronic
or mechanical, including photocopying, recording, taping or
information storage and retrieval systems – without the
prior permission in writing of the publishers.

This book is produced using paper that is made from wood
grown in managed, sustainable forests. It is natural, renewable
and recyclable. The logging and manufacturing processes conform
to the environmental regulations of the country of origin.

Printed and bound in China by C&C Offset Printing Co.

# Chapter One

It was Monday morning. Lara was in the kitchen, putting an apple in her lunch box.

Lara's tabby cat rubbed round her legs. Lara put some food in Tiggy's bowl.

Tiggy purred. She needed to eat lots of food. She was going to have kittens soon.

Lara looked at the clock.

"Hurry up, Mum! It's time to go to school," she called.

Mum was busy, painting at the table.

"Just one more minute!" she said.

"It's time to go *now*, Mum!" Lara said.

It took Lara and Mum ten minutes to walk to school. The children were already lining up in the playground.

"Just in time, Lara!" Miss Button said. "Quiet, everyone! Coats on pegs, lunch boxes on the trolley. Then go and sit on the mat."

Lara hung her coat on her peg.
But OH NO! Where was her lunch box?

Lara remembered putting the apple inside. But the lunch box was still on the kitchen table.

Lara went to sit on the mat.

"What's the matter, Lara?" asked Miss Button.

"I've forgotten my lunch," Lara said.

"Never mind," Miss Button said. "You can have school dinner, just for today."

Miss Button called the register. Lara
remembered to listen for her name and say
"Yes, Miss Button".

It was Zak's turn to take the register to
the school office.

Molly did the calendar.

Next, they wrote in their News books.

Lara stared out of the window. The tree was full of birds.

"Stop daydreaming please, Lara," Miss Button said.

Lara didn't know what to write. She stared out of the window again. She thought about her cat.

My cat Tiggy is going to have kittens, Lara wrote in her News book.

At last it was time for lunch.

"Pizza or pasta?" Miss Button asked.

"Pasta, please," Lara said. She ate slowly.
She didn't like it very much.

Here," Zak said. "Have half my sandwich."
Molly gave Lara her apple.

At home time, Miss Button said, "What do you need to remember tomorrow, Lara?"

"My lunch box?" Lara said.

"Yes. And to stop daydreaming!"

Lara sighed. There was so much to remember at school.

# Chapter Two

On Tuesday morning, Mum made Lara's lunch. Lara fed Tiggy.

"It's my turn to do the calendar today," Lara told Mum.

"We'll try to be early, then," Mum said.

Lara picked up her lunch box. Then Lara and Mum skipped down the road.

At school, Lara did the calendar.

Today is TUESDAY 2nd. The month is MARCH. The weather is SUNNY.

"Well done, Lara," Miss Button said.

Next, they did adding and taking away numbers.

Lara looked out of the window. She thought about her cat. Perhaps Tiggy would have three kittens. One cat add three kittens made four.

"Lara?" said Miss Button. "Pay attention, please."

After lunch, it was time for reading.

"Fetch your book bags," Miss Button said.

Lara went to her drawer to find her book.

"OH NO!" she said. "I've left my book bag at home!"

"Never mind," Molly said. "You can share my book."

Lara and Molly read the story together. It was about a dog called Harry.

At home time, Miss Button said, "Tomorrow, remember your lunch box *and* your book bag, please, Lara. And don't forget the new words in your spelling tin. That's *three* things to remember!"

Granny collected Lara because Mum was in the middle of a painting.

"How was school today?" Granny asked.

"I forgot my book bag," Lara said. "There are too many things to remember."

After tea, Granny helped Lara learn the new words in her spelling tin. They spread them out on the table. Lara liked the words *kitten* and *pretty* best.

# Chapter Three

On Wednesday morning, Tiggy ate two breakfasts.

Lara put her spelling tin into her book bag. She picked up her lunch box.

"Hurry up, Mum!" she said.

They got to school just as Miss Button rang the bell.

When it was time to do spellings, Lara went to get her tin of words. But OH NO! The tin was empty!

Lara remembered looking at the words on the table with Granny. She must have left them there!

"Never mind," Zak said. "You can share my words."

But Zak's words were different. Zak's words were *cat* and *sit* and *mat*.

"I had *pretty* and *kitten* and *little*," Lara said. She wrote down the words to show him.

"Well, it's good you have remembered how to spell the words," Miss Button said. "Even if you forgot to bring them in!"

Lara felt happier. "Any day now," she told Zak, "Tiggy will have her kittens."

Molly and Zak wanted one each.

They made a list of names for them.

KITTEN NAMES:
- Midnight
- Shadow
- Tiger
- Kitty
- Mittens
- Moon
- Boo

"A list is a good way to remember things," Miss Button said to Lara at home time. "Put *plimsolls* on your list for tomorrow."

# Chapter Four

On Thursday morning, Lara sat at the kitchen table. She wrote:

things I need for school:
- Book bag
- Lunch box
- Spelling tin with new words (Wednesday)
- Plimsolls (thursday)

Mum stuck the list on the fridge.

Tiggy prowled round the kitchen, mewing.

"I think she will have her kittens today," Mum said.

Lara hopped up and down in excitement.

"Are you ready for school?" Mum asked.

Lara checked her list. "Yes," she said.

"I think I've remembered everything!"

All day, Lara thought about the kittens.
She stared out of the window. She didn't
listen to what Miss Button was saying.
"Lara? You're daydreaming again!"
Miss Button said.

After lunch, in science, they put beans on to a bed of cotton wool in a jar and watered them. They were going to find out which came first, the roots or the tiny new shoots.

But OH NO! Lara knocked her jar off the windowsill by mistake and made a big mess.

"Sorry," Lara said.

"Never mind," Molly said.

She helped Lara clean up the mess.

"Tomorrow you will need your painting aprons," Miss Button said at home time. "DON'T FORGET, Lara!'

Mum was waiting in the playground.

"Have the kittens been born?" Lara asked.

"Not yet!" Mum said.

# Chapter Five

On Friday morning, Lara came into the kitchen. Tiggy was curled up in a box under the table. Lara knelt down to look inside.

"AHHHH!" Lara said.

There were three tiny kittens in the box! One was black, one was grey and one was tabby, like Tiggy.

Lara remembered the list of names she had made with Molly and Zak. She chose three.

Midnight for
the black kitten.

Shadow for
the grey kitten.

Tiger for the
tabby kitten.

"Time for school," Mum said.
Lara looked
at her list.

things I need for school:
· Book bag
· Lunch box
· Spelling tin with
new words
(Wednesday)
· Plimsolls
(Thursday)

· Painting apron
(Friday)

Today was Friday, so she needed her apron. But she couldn't find it anywhere!

"That's odd," Mum said. "But I've got an idea…" She knelt down and looked inside the box of kittens. "Guess what? I think Tiggy has borrowed your apron to make a nest!"

Lara laughed.

"Tell your teacher about the kittens," Mum said. "And you can borrow my big apron, for painting."

In Show and Tell, Lara told Class 2 about
the new kittens and her apron.
Everyone laughed, even Miss Button.

After lunch, when it was time for painting, Lara stared out of the window. In her head, she saw the picture she wanted to paint – Tiggy and the three kittens curled up on her apron in the box. Lara worked hard, painting her picture. In the end, it looked brilliant!

Miss Button was pleased as well. At home time, she showed it to Lara's mum. "Lara has a real talent," Miss Button said. "Perhaps she will be an artist one day, like you."

Mum laughed. "Yes. An artist and a daydreamer, too!"